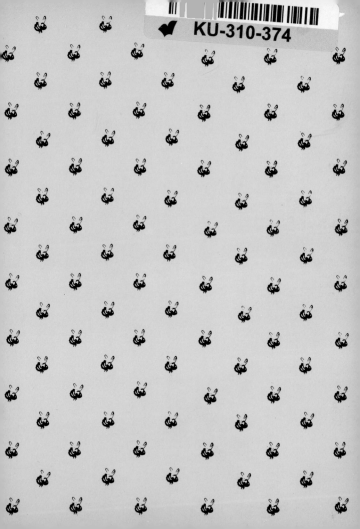

TIGGER IS
UNBOUNCED

TIGGER IS UNBOUNCED

A. A. MILNE

illustrated by

ERNEST H. SHEPARD

TIGGER IS UNBOUNCED

One day Rabbit and Piglet were sitting
outside Pooh's front door listening to
Rabbit, and Pooh was sitting with them.
It was a drowsy summer afternoon, and
the Forest was full of gentle sounds,
which all seemed to be saying to Pooh,
'Don't listen to Rabbit, listen to me.'
So he got into a comfortable position for

not listening to Rabbit, and from time
to time he opened his eyes to say 'Ah!'
and then closed them again to say 'True,'
and from time to time Rabbit said, 'You
see what I mean, Piglet,' very earnestly,
and Piglet nodded earnestly to show that
he did.

'In fact,' said Rabbit, coming to the
end of it at last, 'Tigger's getting so
Bouncy nowadays that it's time we taught
him a lesson. Don't you think so, Piglet?'

Piglet said that Tigger *was* very
Bouncy, and that if they could think of a
way of unbouncing him it would be a Very
Good Idea.

'Just what I feel,' said Rabbit. 'What do *you* say, Pooh?'

Pooh opened his eyes with a jerk and said 'Extremely.'

'Extremely what?' asked Rabbit.

'What you were saying,' said Pooh. 'Undoubtably.'

Piglet gave Pooh a stiffening sort of nudge, and Pooh, who felt more and more that he was somewhere else, got up slowly and began to look for himself.

'But how shall we do it?' asked Piglet. 'What sort of a lesson, Rabbit?'

'That's the point,' said Rabbit.

The word 'lesson' came back to Pooh as one he had heard before somewhere.

'There's a thing called Twy-stymes,' he said. 'Christopher Robin tried to teach it to me once, but it didn't.'

'What didn't?' said Rabbit.

'Didn't what?' said Piglet.

Pooh shook his head.

'I don't know,' he said. 'It just didn't. What are we talking about?'

'Pooh,' said Piglet reproachfully, 'haven't you been listening to what Rabbit was saying?'

'I listened, but I had a small piece of fluff in my ear. Could you say it again, please, Rabbit?'

Rabbit never minded saying things again, so he asked where he should begin from; and when Pooh had said from the moment when the fluff got in his ear, and Rabbit had asked when that was, and Pooh had said he didn't know because he hadn't heard properly, Piglet settled it all by saying that what they were trying to do was, they were just trying to think of a way to get the bounces out of Tigger, because however much you liked him, you couldn't deny it, he *did* bounce.

'Oh, I see,' said Pooh.

'There's too much of him,' said Rabbit,

'that's what it comes to.'

Pooh tried to think, and all he could think
of was something which didn't help at all.
So he hummed it very quietly to himself.

If Rabbit
Was bigger
And fatter
And stronger,
Or bigger
Than Tigger,
If Tigger was smaller,
Then Tigger's bad habit
Of bouncing at Rabbit
Would matter
No longer,
If Rabbit
Was taller.

'What was Pooh saying?' asked Rabbit.
'Any good?'

'No,' said Pooh sadly. 'No good.'

'Well, I've got an idea,' said Rabbit,
'and here it is. We take Tigger for a long

explore, somewhere where he's never been, and we lose him there, and next morning we find him again, and—mark my words—he'll be a different Tigger altogether.'

'Why?' said Pooh.

'Because he'll be a Humble Tigger. Because he'll be a Sad Tigger, a Melancholy Tigger, a Small and Sorry Tigger, an Oh-Rabbit-I-*am*-glad-to-see-you Tigger. That's why.'

'Will he be glad to see me and Piglet, too?'

'Of course.'

'That's good,' said Pooh.

'I should hate him to go *on* being Sad,' said Piglet doubtfully.

'Tiggers never go on being Sad,' explained

Rabbit. 'They get over it with Astonishing Rapidity. I asked Owl, just to make sure, and he said that that's what they always get over it with. But if we can make

Tigger feel Small and Sad just for five minutes, we shall have done a good deed.'

'Would Christopher Robin think so?' asked Piglet.

'Yes,' said Rabbit. 'He'd say "You've done a good deed, Piglet. I would have done it myself, only I happened to be doing something else. Thank you, Piglet." And Pooh, of course.'

Piglet felt very glad about this, and he saw at once that what they were going to do to Tigger was a good thing to do, and as Pooh and Rabbit were doing it with him, it was a thing which even a Very Small Animal could wake up in the morning and be comfortable about doing. So the only question was, where should they lose Tigger?

'We'll take him to the North Pole,' said Rabbit, 'because it was a very long explore finding it, so it will be a very long explore for Tigger un-finding it again.'

It was now Pooh's turn to feel very glad,

because it was he who had first found the
North Pole, and when they got there, Tigger
would see a notice which said, 'Discovered
by Pooh, Pooh found it,' and then Tigger
would know, which perhaps he didn't now,
the sort of Bear Pooh was. *That* sort of Bear.

So it was arranged that they should
start next morning, and that Rabbit, who
lived near Kanga and Roo and Tigger, should
now go home and ask Tigger what he was
doing to-morrow, because if he wasn't doing
anything, what about coming for an explore
and getting Pooh and Piglet to come too?
And if Tigger said 'Yes' that would be all
right, and if he said 'No'—

'He won't,' said Rabbit. 'Leave it to me.'
And he went off busily.

The next day was quite a different day.
Instead of being hot and sunny, it was cold
and misty. Pooh didn't mind for himself,
but when he thought of all the honey the bees
wouldn't be making, a cold and misty day

always made him feel sorry for them. He said
so to Piglet when Piglet came to fetch him,
and Piglet said that he wasn't thinking of
that so much, but of how cold and miserable
it would be being lost all day and night on
the top of the Forest. But when he and Pooh
had got to Rabbit's house, Rabbit said it
was just the day for them, because Tigger
always bounced on ahead of everybody, and
as soon as he got out of sight, they would
hurry away in the other direction, and he
would never see them again.

'Not never?' said Piglet.

'Well, not until we find him again,

Piglet. To-morrow, or whenever it is. Come on. He's waiting for us.'

When they got to Kanga's house, they found that Roo was waiting too, being a great friend of Tigger's, which made it Awkward; but Rabbit whispered 'Leave this to me' behind his paw to Pooh, and went up to Kanga.

'I don't think Roo had better come,' he said. 'Not to-day.'

'Why not?' said Roo, who wasn't supposed to be listening.

'Nasty cold day,' said Rabbit, shaking his head. 'And you were coughing this morning.'

'How do you know?' asked Roo indignantly.

'Oh, Roo, you never told me,' said Kanga reproachfully.

'It was a biscuit cough,' said Roo, 'not one to tell about.'

'I think not to-day, dear. Another day.'

'To-morrow?' said Roo hopefully.

'We'll see,' said Kanga.

'You're always seeing and nothing ever

happens,' said Roo sadly.

'Nobody could see on a day like this,
Roo,' said Rabbit. 'I don't expect we shall
get very far, and then this afternoon we'll
all—we'll all—we'll—ah, Tigger, there
you are. Come on. Good-bye, Roo! This
afternoon we'll—come on, Pooh! All ready?
That's right. Come on.'

So they went. At first Pooh and Rabbit
and Piglet walked together, and Tigger ran
round them in circles, and then, when the

path got narrower, Rabbit, Piglet and Pooh walked one after another, and Tigger ran round them in oblongs, and by-and-by, when the gorse got very prickly on each side of the path, Tigger ran up and down in front of them,

and sometimes he bounced into Rabbit and sometimes he didn't. And as they got higher, the mist got thicker, so that Tigger kept disappearing, and then when you thought he wasn't there, there he was again, saying, 'I say, come on,' and before you could say anything, there he wasn't.

Rabbit turned round and nudged Piglet.

'The next time,' he said. 'Tell Pooh.'

'The next time,' said Piglet to Pooh.

'The next what?' said Pooh to Piglet.

Tigger appeared suddenly, bounced into Rabbit, and disappeared again. 'Now!' said Rabbit. He jumped into a hollow by the side of the path, and Pooh and Piglet jumped after him. They crouched in the bracken, listening. The Forest was very silent when you stopped and listened to it. They could see nothing and hear nothing.

'H'sh!' said Rabbit.

'I am,' said Pooh.

There was a pattering noise . . . then silence again.

'Hallo!' said Tigger, and he sounded so close suddenly that Piglet would have jumped if Pooh hadn't accidentally been sitting on most of him.

'Where are you?' called Tigger.

Rabbit nudged Pooh, and Pooh looked about for Piglet to nudge, but couldn't find him, and Piglet went on breathing wet bracken as quietly as he could, and felt very brave and excited.

'That's funny,' said Tigger.

There was a moment's silence, and then they heard him pattering off again. For a little longer they waited, until the

Forest had become so still that it almost frightened them, and then Rabbit got up and stretched himself.

'Well?' he whispered proudly. 'There we are! Just as I said.'

'I've been thinking,' said Pooh, 'and I think—'

'No,' said Rabbit. 'Don't. Run. Come on.' And they all hurried off, Rabbit leading the way.

'Now,' said Rabbit, after they had gone a little way, 'we can talk. What were you going to say, Pooh?'

'Nothing much. Why are we going along here?'

'Because it's the way home.'

'Oh!' said Pooh.

'I *think* it's more to the right,' said Piglet nervously. 'What do *you* think, Pooh?'

Pooh looked at his two paws. He knew that one of them was the right, and he knew that when you had decided which one of them was the right, then the other one was the left, but he never could remember how to begin.

'Well—' he said slowly.

'Come on,' said Rabbit. 'I know it's this way.'

They went on. Ten minutes later they stopped again.

'It's very silly,' said Rabbit, 'but just for the moment I—Ah, of course. Come on.' . . .

'Here we are,' said Rabbit ten minutes later. 'No, we're not.' . . .

'Now,' said Rabbit ten minutes later, 'I think we ought to be getting—or are we a little bit more to the right than I thought?' . . .

'It's a funny thing,' said Rabbit ten minutes later, 'how everything looks the same in a mist. Have you noticed it, Pooh?'

Pooh said that he had.

'Lucky we know the Forest so well, or we

might get lost,' said Rabbit half an hour later, and he gave the careless laugh which you give when you know the Forest so well that you can't get lost.

Piglet sidled up to Pooh from behind.

'Pooh!' he whispered.

'Yes, Piglet?'

'Nothing,' said Piglet, taking Pooh's paw. 'I just wanted to be sure of you.'

When Tigger had finished waiting for the others to catch him up, and they hadn't, and when he had got tired of having nobody to say 'I say, come on' to, he thought he would go home. So he trotted back; and the first thing Kanga said when she saw him was, 'There's a good Tigger. You're just in time for your Strengthening Medicine,' and she poured it out for him. Roo said proudly, 'I've *had* mine,' and Tigger swallowed his and said, 'So have I,' and then he and Roo pushed each other about in a friendly way, and Tigger accidentally knocked over one or two chairs by accident, and Roo accidentally knocked over one on purpose, and Kanga said, 'Now then, run along.'

'Where shall we run along to?' asked Roo.

'You can go and collect some fir-cones for me,' said Kanga, giving them a basket.

So they went to the Six Pine Trees, and threw fir-cones at each other until they had forgotten what they came for, and they left the basket under the trees and went back to dinner. And it was just as they were finishing dinner that Christopher Robin put his head in at the door.

'Where's Pooh?' he asked.

'Tigger dear, where's Pooh?' said Kanga. Tigger explained what had happened at the same time that Roo was explaining about his Biscuit Cough and Kanga was telling them not both to talk at once, so it was some time before Christopher Robin guessed that Pooh and Piglet and Rabbit were all lost in the

mist on the top of the Forest.

'It's a funny thing about Tiggers,' whispered Tigger to Roo, 'how Tiggers *never* get lost.'

'Why don't they, Tigger?'

'They just don't,' explained Tigger. 'That's how it is.'

'Well,' said Christopher Robin, 'we shall have to go and find them, that's all. Come on, Tigger.'

'I shall have to go and find them,' explained Tigger to Roo.

'May I find them too?' asked Roo eagerly.

'I think not to-day, dear,' said Kanga. 'Another day.'

'Well, if they're lost to-morrow, may I find them?'

'We'll see,' said Kanga, and Roo, who knew what *that* meant, went into a corner and practised jumping out at himself, partly because he wanted to practise this, and partly because he didn't want Christopher Robin and Tigger to think that he minded when they went off without him.

'The fact is,' said Rabbit, 'we've missed our way somehow.'

They were having a rest in a small sand-pit on the top of the Forest. Pooh was getting rather tired of that sand-pit, and suspected it of following them about, because whichever direction they started in, they always ended up at it, and each time, as it came through the mist at them, Rabbit said triumphantly, 'Now I know where we are!' and Pooh said sadly, 'So do I,' and Piglet

said nothing. He had tried to think of something
to say, but the only thing he could think of was,
'Help, help!' and it seemed silly to say that,
when he had Pooh and Rabbit with him.

'Well,' said Rabbit, after a long silence in
which nobody thanked him for the nice walk they
were having, 'we'd better get on, I suppose.
Which way shall we try?'

'How would it be,' said Pooh slowly, 'if
as soon as we're out of sight of this Pit, we
try to find it again?'

'What's the good of that?' said Rabbit.

'Well,' said Pooh, 'we keep looking for Home and not finding it, so I thought that if we looked for this Pit we'd be sure not to find it, which would be a Good Thing, because then we might find something that we *weren't* looking for, which might be just what we *were* looking for, really!'

'I don't see much sense in that,' said Rabbit.

'No,' said Pooh humbly, 'there isn't. But there was *going* to be when I began it. It's just that something happened to it on the way.'

'If I walked away from this Pit, and then walked back to it, of *course* I should find it.'

'Well, I thought perhaps you wouldn't,' said Pooh. 'I just thought.'

'Try,' said Piglet suddenly. 'We'll wait here for you.'

Rabbit gave a laugh to show how silly Piglet was, and walked into the mist. After he had gone a hundred yards, he turned and walked back again . . . and after Pooh and Piglet had waited twenty minutes for him Pooh got up.

'I just thought,' said Pooh. 'Now then, Piglet, let's go home.'

'But, Pooh,' cried Piglet, all excited, 'do you know the way?'

'No,' said Pooh. 'But there are twelve pots of honey in my cupboard, and they've been calling to me for hours. I couldn't hear them properly before because Rabbit *would* talk, but if nobody says anything except those twelve pots, I *think*, Piglet, I shall know where they're coming from. Come on.'

They walked off together; and for a long time Piglet said nothing, so as not to interrupt the pots; and then suddenly he made a squeaky noise...and an oo-noise ...because now he began to know where he was; but he still didn't dare to say so out loud, in case he wasn't. And just when he was getting so sure of himself that it didn't matter whether the pots went on calling or not, there was a shout from in front of them,

and out of the mist came Christopher Robin.

'Oh, there you are,' said Christopher Robin
carelessly, trying to pretend that he hadn't
been Anxious.

'Here we are,' said Pooh.

'Where's Rabbit?'

'I don't know,' said Pooh.

'Oh — well, I expect Tigger will find him.
He's sort of looking for you all.'

'Well,' said Pooh, 'I've got to go home for something, and so has Piglet, because we haven't had it yet, and—'

'I'll come and watch you,' said Christopher Robin.

So he went home with Pooh, and watched him for quite a long time . . . and all the time he was

watching, Tigger was tearing round the Forest making loud yapping noises for Rabbit. And at last a very Small and Sorry Rabbit heard him. And the Small and Sorry Rabbit rushed through the mist at the noise, and it suddenly turned into Tigger; a Friendly Tigger, a Grand Tigger, a Large and Helpful Tigger, a Tigger who bounced, if he bounced at all, in just the beautiful way a Tigger ought to bounce.

'Oh, Tigger, I *am* glad to see you,' cried Rabbit.

Tigger is Unbounced
is taken from *The House at Pooh Corner*
originally published in
Great Britain 11 October 1928
by Methuen & Co. Ltd
Text by A.A.Milne and line drawings by Ernest H. Shepard
copyright under the Berne Convention

This book club edition first published by Grolier 1995
Published by arrangement with Egmont Children's Books Limited
Reprinted 1999

First published in this edition 1991
by Methuen Children's Books
an imprint of Egmont Children's Books Limited
239 Kensington High Street, London W8 6SA

Printed in Hong Kong

ISBN 0 416 17172 9